For Abbe

Library of Congress Cataloging-in-Publication Data.
Stock, Catherine.   Easter surprise   /   by Catherine
Stock.   —   1st ed.   p.   cm.   Summary: A
brother and sister spend Easter with their mother in a little cabin on the lake.   ISBN 0-02-788371-X   [1. Easter—
Fiction.]   I. Title.   PZ7.S8635Eas   1991   [E]—dc20
90-1915   CIP   AC

Easter Surprise

BY CATHERINE STOCK

BRADBURY PRESS · NEW YORK

COLLIER MACMILLAN CANADA
Toronto
MAXWELL MACMILLAN INTERNATIONAL PUBLISHING GROUP
New York   Oxford   Singapore   Sydney

My daffodil has opened.
It's spring.

My brother Max stays home
because it's the school holidays.

We're going to Stocking Heel Lake for the weekend.

Miss Brown next door will feed Rhubarb, our cat.

"If we're lucky, we might see the Easter Bunny in the country," says Mommy.

We are staying in a little cabin
on the lake.
    There are bunk beds in the room.
Max takes the top bunk and I take
the bottom bunk.

I put on my pajamas and brush my teeth.

"Not those books," I tell Mommy. "Tell me a story about the Easter Bunny."

The next morning we decorate
eggs with colored paints.
   Max paints an orange dot on
his nose.

Mommy ties a new yellow ribbon on my sunbonnet and we go rowing on the lake.

The sun squints on the water.

"I can't see any bunnies," I say.

"Bunnies don't swim, silly," says Max.

The next day is Easter.

It's time for the Easter egg hunt.

Max looks in some bushes and finds a chocolate egg wrapped in silver paper!

Then he finds a marzipan duck
and a chocolate rabbit.

I can't find anything.

Mommy helps me.

She tells me that I'm getting warm when I get closer to something.

I find a little basket of sugar eggs!

"Warmer, warmer, hot, hot, hot!"

I find a new pink toy mouse with a bell for Rhubarb!

Then I find a chocolate bunny with a pink ribbon.

"You're my Easter Bunny," I whisper to Mommy that night.

Mommy smiles. "And you and Max are my all-year bunnies," she whispers back.